Days of Plenty, Days of Want

Camino del Sol

A Chicana and Chicano Literary Series

Days of Plenty, Days of Want

Patricia Preciado Martin

The University of Arizona Press   Tucson

©1988 by Bilingual Press/Editorial Bilingüe
First University of Arizona Press paperbound edition 1999
All rights reserved
♾ This book is printed on acid-free, archival-quality paper.
Manufactured in the United States of America

04 03 02 01 00 99 6 5 4 3 2 1

Library of Congress Cataloging-in-Publication Data
Martin, Patricia Preciado
Days of plenty, days of want / Patricia Preciado Martin.
p. cm. — (Camino del Sol)
ISBN 0-8165-1946-3 (pbk.)
1. Mexican Americans—Social life and customs—Fiction.
I. Title. II. Series.
PS3563.A7272D39 1999
813'.54—dc21   98-46458

British Library Cataloguing-in-Publication Data
A catalogue record for this book is available from the British Library.

Contents

Dedicated to Jim, Elenita, and Jimmy,
in gratitude for the love and the laughter.

The Clear Voice of Heritage

Carmen Tafolla

In the writings of Patricia Preciado Martin, one hears the clear voice of heritage. This is not a heritage that comes as an artifact disinterred and rediscovered, but rather it is an intimate treasure mirrored generation upon generation and passed spirit to spirit in an undying breath of life. As the reader moves through her stories there is at once a sense of timelessness and absolute rootedness. The stories move from the past to the present and back to the past with no change of tone or clarity. To Preciado Martin, the past is every bit as real as the present, and every bit as pervasive and all-encompassing.

In some stories, this is painted clearly and in sequence ("Days of Plenty, Days of Want" and "Journey"). In others, the simultaneity of past and present is artistically woven into a haunting tone that never leaves us, while reminding us that the past never leaves us either. This flexibility with the sequence of time reminds us of similar approaches in 20th-century Latin American novels, but in these stories it is less a tool of artistic style than an integration in concept.

Also reminiscent of Latin American literature is a hint of magical realism in the strange and oddly symbolic events that manifest themselves as plot resolutions. For instance, in the powerful and haunting "Ruins," the aging Doña Luz had recorded, on hundreds of shreds of paper,

> the history of our people which I have gath-
> ered—the land grants and the homesteads and
> the property transfers . . . the deeds, honorable
> and dishonorable; the baptisms, the weddings,
> the funerals; the prayers and processions and the
> santos to whom they are directed . . . the mila-
> gros and the superstitions. . . . The recipes, the
> herbs and the cures; the music and the songs and
> the dances; the prose and the poems, the sor-
> rows, the joys; the gain and the loss.

In a magical summary of reality, these messages in the hands
of Alma (the soul) fly from her grasp with the wind that has
blown open the door and become "giant white moths." And we,
as readers, stand in as much amazement as Alma, our soul, when

> Blowing snow mingled with blowing paper and
> rose and fell and then eddied into a blizzard of
> memories. And then the memories and the spirit
> of Doña Luz fluttered out the open door in a
> thousand swirling fragments in the direction of
> the south wind somewhere west of Aztlán.

There is a natural order, a sense of victory and openness, as all
these messages fly off into the hearts of readers. There is also a
sense of magic that is too intimate to be anything less than real.

It is not surprising that the elements of history and legacy
should surface in the writings of Patricia Preciado Martin. Born
in Prescott, Arizona, and raised in Tucson, she not only lived in
the Chicano barrios and ranchos that begat her characters but
also actively collected folklore and local history as an adult and
served as a consultant to numerous history projects dealing with
the Mexican-American presence in the Southwest.

A magna cum laude graduate of the University of Arizona,
Preciado Martin has been the guest curator of the Arizona Historical Society's Mexican Heritage Project since 1982. Her first

book was a children's book, *Legend of the Bellringer of San Agustín* (1982), and this was followed in 1983 by a collection of notes and portraits entitled *Images and Conversations: Mexican Americans Recall a Southwestern Past.* In this work, her sensitivity to person and place becomes evident. A natural folklorist, she enhances her interviews with the deeper understanding that allows the reader to capture the speakers' faces and words and, more importantly, what lies between their words: their personal victories and tragedies, their values, their passions—in essence, their spirit.

She describes this time of collecting oral histories in the homes and barrios of Tucson as having planted the ideas for her later short stories. "They are stories whose seeds were sown by the lives of our people," she writes, "humble people of great faith whose unspoken dreams and hopes gave wing to my imagination." The years of interviewing were only the trigger that set off what had been happening in her for many years as she observed the people of the barrios, most significant among them for their influence her mother, Aurelia, and her mother's friend, Doña Rosa. "For more years than I can remember," she explains, "their humble adobe homes and their kitchen tables and home altars were the focus of my daily life." She puts this familiarity and this understanding to good use in her narrative of the lives of the real figures in *Images and Conversations.* In the voices of the people of Southern Arizona, she finds a work of documentary poetry.

In *Days of Plenty, Days of Want,* Preciado Martin has carried that sense of the poetic and that familiarity with the heart of her community into a fiction that is every bit as real and stunning to our hearts and minds as the earlier interview/narratives. In some ways, the stories become more real than non-fiction, for they epitomize and summarize the thoughts and experiences of a people as few individual lives can. In "María de las Trenzas," for example, María seems to carry a multitude of burdens and to fulfill each of a myriad of expectations of different people regarding her role. Yet her escapes of fancy, too, wear many different faces. And when she at last frees herself in that very symbolic

severing of the repetitive woven pattern of her hair—the symbolic dutifulness, restraint, and constancy of her very predictable
braids—we seem to sense the victory and the freedom of not one
person, but many. She has left behind the one person, María de
las Trenzas, predictable as others' expectations, solid and tangi-
ble and smooth-lined as the clean braids on the table, "cut neatly
from the nape of her neck." Her hair is now loose, with a thousand strands of possibilities and directions, and unbraided as in
all her fantasies. The many lives she is now free to live are our
multiple victors.

In stories such as "María de las Trenzas," "Dreams," and
"Earth to Earth," Preciado Martin displays her finest art: characterization so careful as to qualify as literary portraiture. Like other
Chicana writers—Yolanda Luera, Teresa Acosta, Sylviana
Wood—her characterizations are strong and echo off the page
and into reality. They form portraits that entice all the senses
and that capture spirit and desire in their description. The pro-
tagonist in "Dreams," for example, emanates past and present
simultaneously:

> . . . like a door slightly ajar to a dimly lit room
> full of secrets. . . . He would eat slowly, deliber-
> ately, hunched over, intent on his plate, as silent
> and immovable as one of the apostles in the dime
> store print of the Last Supper that graced the
> wall above the kitchen table. . . .
>
> The chair . . . the only heirloom . . . had been
> made to order for his tall and angular frame, but
> the years and pendientes and his losses had
> shrunk Tata's bones and he seemed lost, wizened
> and childlike in the oversized throne. Nonethe-
> less, there he sat and surveyed his diminutive
> kingdom and brooded about his lost youth and
> strength . . .
>
> . . . At the far end of the lot, under a salt-dusted
> tamarack was a ramshackle chicken coop inhab-

ited by a one-eyed rooster with an evil disposition and his harem of forlorn hens in various
stages of pecked disarray. Tata Elías kept watch
over the motley flock as if they were a herd of
high-strung racehorses or prize cattle. Every
morning an egg or two or three would miraculously materialize . . . no one was allowed to
enter the coop or gather the eggs but him. They
were for his consumption alone: his manna from
heaven, the bounty of his harvest, pearls of great
price, the only precious stones remaining in the
diadem of his monotonous days.

The portrait and the setting are so enveloping that Preciado
Martin manages to entrance us even in a story like "Dreams,"
where there is no active plot and little character development,
but only the revelation of character, that slow opening of a door
to a "dimly lit room full of secrets." It is at the inspiration of such
characters that the poetic eloquence of her prose rises to its best:
"And the days rolled by like beads of rainwater on a pane, and
the days pooled into the nostalgic corners of his mind and
drowned him with his memories."

This concern with poetic description and character over ac-
tion might not win critical approval for these stories within
modern American literature. While poetic eloquence was of
high priority in the earlier traditions of American prose, it is not
the current rage. The style of preference in contemporary American literature is much barer, much more involved with small
symbolic actions or large fast-paced ones. In American literature
of this century, we have become increasingly enamored of the
Shaker tradition, that of simple functionalism and sparsity of
detail. In this respect, Preciado Martin is more easily compared
to contemporary Latin American writers, where there is less
discomfort with both emotion and poetic prose. But the great
concern with whether Chicano literature fits more appropriately
within American literature or Latin American literature is typi-
cally a useless debate, for Chicano literature rightly contains

elements of both traditions, and Preciado Martin's works are no exception.

In most of her stories, Preciado Martin combines strong characterization with a careful line of plot that displays change, lack of change, and irony. In "Days of Plenty, Days of Want," past and present reflect each other in two characters of similar temperament, inclination, and destiny. History repeats itself with only a slight change of name and props. And Preciado Martin's message is heard once more—heritage. Heritage is the key to who and what we are now. In "Earth to Earth" we see part of that heritage destroyed, but not without a struggle and not without its own form of victory. In "The Farewell" we see heritage being cramped and changed against the will of its bearers by a society that does not respect heritage as much as property. In "The Journey" we see ultimate victory. The more things change, the more they stay the same. The heritage is carried on. The flowers resurface through the cracked asphalt. And the message seems to return to the beginning: the "white butterflies" of paper from "The Ruins" are carried on the wind of our hearts and never disappear to the eyes of the spirit. That which rises from the ruins is that which lasts— our legacy, our essence.

In summary, the collection *Days of Plenty, Days of Want* goes beyond the legends and the folklore, though these are included as an integral part of the stories themselves. It goes beyond being a loose handful of well-wrought but separate stories, several of which have been individual award winners in national competitions. This collection fits together from beginning to end, in style and sequence and in underlying message. It shapes a special voice and emanates a special spirit. It carries the heritage, the undying spirit, which passes from one person to the next and one century to the next. It is not artificial, with forced or contrived characters. No, these stories have walked and lived and cried and aged and died . . . and have, always, left their heritage.

Dr. Carmen Tafolla is a writer and educational consultant and has taught at numerous educational institutions throughout the Southwest.

Days of Plenty, Days of Want

The Ruins

It was getting so that almost every day Alma was going to the ruins on the riverbank. Not that her mother knew, of course. She was expressly forbidden to go there. It was a place, her mother Mercedes warned, that winos went on occasion, and young lovers, frequently. One never knew what kind of mischief or carnal knowledge one might come upon or witness. When Señora Romero spoke like this—of the proximity of temptation or occasions of sin—she would finger the large gold medallion of the Sagrado Corazón that she wore around her neck and invoke protection for her oldest daughter from the phalanx of saints with which she was on a first name basis. The image of the Sagrado Corazón was fortified on the reverse side with an engraving of the Virgen de Guadalupe, and Señora Romero wore the medal like the medieval armor of a crusader prepared to do battle with the infidel. It was a pose Alma saw her mother strike with frequency—inspired by the worldliness promoted by newspapers, television, popular music, protestantes and errant in-laws.

(She was not being disrespectful, Alma had convinced herself, when her mother would begin her pious sermons, to imagine Doña Mercedes, a fury on a rearing stallion—lance raised, mail clanking, banners aloft—routing unbelievers and sinners from the cantinas and alleyways of South Tucson, until they knelt trembling and repentant at the vestibule of Santa Cruz Church. Sra. Romero mistook Alma's dreamy unwavering stare for attentiveness, and so these periodic encounters left all parties satisfied. In reality, Sra. Romero never behaved in any manner that would have called attention to herself: decorum, simplicity and moderation were the measures by which she lived her life and by which she ruled her family.)

It was easy enough for Alma to keep her afternoon sojourns secret from her mother. The excuses were varied and plentiful: extra homework in the library, a dance committee, an after-school game or conference with a teacher. In truth, there was never anything or anyone at school that attracted Alma's attention or detained her there. She was a solitary and thoughtful girl—dutiful in her studies, retiring in her behavior, guarded in her conversation—and so she went unnoticed by her teachers and ignored by the giggling groups of friends that gathered in animated knots in the halls, in the cafeteria and on the school grounds.

(Alma seemed plain to the casual observer. Her dress was modest, almost dowdy, created from cheap fabric by the nimble fingers of her mother on her Singer treadle sewing machine. She wore no makeup or jewelry, in contrast to her peers at school: with their brightly colored clothes and lips, patterned stockings and flashy plastic accessories, they swarmed through the halls like flocks of rainbow-hued wingless birds. But it could be said that Alma had a certain beauty: she was slim and muscular and lithe, with dark, serious eyes and coppery brown curly hair that obeyed no comb or brush or stylistic whim of her mother. Sra. Romero had long ago given up trying to tame Alma's unruly locks with ribbons and barrettes, abandoning these efforts to dedicate herself to other pursuits that were more pliable to her will.)

Alma always made sure that she arrived home from school at a reasonable hour—in time to help with supper chores or to baby-sit her younger siblings if needed. Sra. Romero never questioned her tardiness or investigated, satisfied that the delay of an hour or sometimes two, was taken up with school activities. A growing family, household duties and spiritual obligations kept Sra. Romero busy enough. It contented her that there were no calls from the principal or teachers, and Alma's excellent grades were testament enough to her industriousness and trustworthiness. All was well.

Sra. Romero prided herself on the fact that her household ran so smoothly, and she credited the personal intervention of the Sagrado Corazón de Jesús for her good fortune. She was a dedicated and energetic woman who scrubbed, polished, cooked, washed, ironed, sewed and prayed with great fervor. Her humble home was spotless, her children orderly, her marriage stable if predictable. Her soul was as spotless as her house, and it was the former that preoccupied her the most—but never (and she was scrupulous on this issue) to the neglect of her domestic duties. Nonetheless, during the week there always seemed to be a funeral, bautismo or velorio to attend; a vigil to keep; a manda to complete; a novena or rosary to recite; a visita to deliver; an altar cloth to iron and mend. And she was grateful for Alma's good-natured helpfulness around the house.

In addition to her weekly obligations, on Sunday mornings Sra. Romero arose faithfully at 5:00 a.m. to go to the Santa Cruz parish hall to help make menudo with the Guadalupanas to sell after all the masses. It was recompense enough for her, that, thanks in part to her pious efforts and sacrifices, the ancient pastor and his ancient barrio church were solvent. She always made sure, however, that she was home by nine o'clock to marshall her immaculate family to church in time to sit in the front pew at the ten o'clock mass. Her energy in matters spiritual seemed boundless, and she was admired, and at times envied, by the other matrons of the southside parish for the sanctity and punctuality demonstrated by her family.

Alma's father, Sr. José Romero, was a patient and thoughtful man who complied with his wife's spiritual and devotional exigencies without complaining. He had a strong faith, in a manner of speaking, although it had developed more out of philosophical musings and awe of the universe than out of any adherence to theological doctrines. Nonetheless, he faithfully attended church when it was required or politic to do so, and he willingly helped out with repairs at the crumbling church and rectory whenever he could find the time.

Sr. Romero was a good provider whose dependability as a mason for the Estes Homes Construction Company kept his family modestly housed, clothed, and fed. He moonlighted at a Whiting Brothers Gas Station for the extras—music lessons, the yearly trip to California, gifts for special occasions. He himself had few material wants, and, having no interest in money matters, he handed over his paycheck to his thrifty and capable wife who wrought miracles, not only with saints, but with his weekly stipend.

Sr. Romero did, however, always manage to set aside a few dollars for himself from his overtime earnings which he lavished on his one passion—books. Whenever he could, he would browse among the stacks in the Carnegie Public Library by the park, and he would often check out as many as a dozen books at a time. But Sr. Romero loved most of all wandering among the dusty aisles of the dimly lit used bookstore in the old section of downtown. He would spend hours, when possible, leafing through the musty yellowed volumes, studying the tables of contents and illustrations, fingering the cracked leather bindings embossed with gold lettering. The proprietor, a laconic, prematurely gray-haired man confined to a wheelchair due to a childhood illness, didn't seem to mind. They never spoke, except in greeting, yet in an indefinable way they were the most intimate of companions. Whenever Sr. Romero had accumulated enough savings, he would buy an antique volume or two, and his book collection had grown to the point that it occupied every available shelf and tabletop in their small home. He had taken to caching his books in cardboard boxes under the beds—as long as he kept them neatly stored his orderly wife did not complain.

Sr. Romero read voraciously—in Spanish as well as in English. He seemed to have no literary preferences—poetry, philosophy, history, the natural sciences, fiction, biography—all he consumed with equal fervor. Night after night, he would read in his easy chair after the house had turned quiet—the younger children tucked in bed with prayer, his saintly wife occupied with her evening devotions. Alma would study her father through the doorway while doing her homework at the kitchen table. At times he would pause in his reading and close his book, a finger keeping his place. He would shut his eyes in meditation, his head in a halo of light and smoke, his patrician face composed. Alma alone knew about the tiny flame that burned in the hidden hearth of his soul, and she understood that the flame would flicker with meaningless chatter. He, in turn, sensed in his favorite daughter the very same embers glowing unattended. There was an unspoken pact between them, and thus they kept their silence.

*   *   *

Alma cut west across the football field, as had become her custom. Her backpack dangled loosely on her shoulders—she had left her books behind in her locker, having finished her homework during the lunch hour. Across the field she could see jostling groups of students heading east—crossing the light on South Twelfth Avenue to play video games in the shopping mall or to hang out with Cokes and cigarettes at the Circle K. The less fortunate who had to ride the school buses were crowding and shoving in lines as they embarked. The bus driver, an angular man with a long-suffering face, whose request for a transfer was still sitting on the principal's desk, hunched over the steering wheel in resignation. Alma could see arms flailing out the window in greeting, or directing paper missles, and she could hear the muffled shouts and catcalls of the students who were good-naturedly elbowing one another for seats.

There was a cut in the chainlink fence by the bleachers at the far end of the field. It had been repaired many times, but it never stayed mended, this section of the fence being the most accessible and least detected place for those students wanting free entry to the football games. Alma stepped through the break in the fence and headed north, parallel with the dry riverbed that cut a wide swath between the highway and the school grounds. There was a faint path, but since it was seldom used, except by her, it was overgrown, and the ankle-high weeds and seeds scratched her legs and imbedded themselves in her socks.

She hurried now, because the late November days were getting shorter, and her mother told time by the proximity of the sun to the horizon. It was not cold, but the weakening sun looked hazy and gave an illusion of winter. A gust of wind portending a change in the weather blew unexpectedly out of the south. Alma shivered and wrapped her ill-fitting cardigan more tightly around herself. The path narrowed gradually as she continued north, angling now slightly west toward the slope where she would descend into the riverbed in order to cross to the opposite bank. A few hundred yards farther and she could see across the river to the old mission orchard on the other side—a tangle of denuded trees—peach, apricot, pomegranate, fig and lemon, leafless now and overgrown with wild grape and the vines of the morning glory and the buffalo gourd. On the periphery of the abandoned orchard, the silhouettes of two dead cottonwoods thrust their giant trunks into the sky as if in failed supplication for water. By now Alma could see the decaying walls of the ancient adobe convento, and she could discern the elusive wisp of smoke that arose from somewhere amid the ruins. Far to the southeast, in the direction of the Santa Rita Mountains, she could now see dark clouds dragging their heavy burden over the mountain peaks. If the wind quickened, the storm would be here before dusk.

Alma walked faster now, scrambling down one side of the dry river's eroded bank and up the other, artfully sidestepping the litter of flash flood debris, the broken glass and shiny aluminum of beer busts, discarded construction material and abandoned furniture and car parts. When she had reached the other side of the bank, she brushed her way through a stand of scraggly carrizo and walked over a plank suspended over a narrow ragged cut where the river had meandered decades ago. At last she reached the neglected and overgrown orchard that had become her musing, and lately, her observation place. The trees were gnarled with age and barren now, but even in the spring they boasted few leaves, having to depend on the sparse and unpredictable desert rains for their irrigation. It was nothing short of a wonder that they were still alive: each season seemed to be their last, but now the native shrubs and vines had so intertwined themselves with their sorrowful hosts that they seemed perennially, unnaturally, green.

It was here within view of the ruins that Alma had chosen her secret hiding place: here she would sit day after day on a discarded car seat with broken springs that she had laboriously hauled up from the riverbed. It was from this vantage point that she would observe the comings and goings of the strange old woman who had taken up residence in the crumbling site. They had never spoken, but Alma was sure that the old woman was aware of her presence, and at times she thrilled with the sure knowledge that she, also, was being watched at a distance. It was just a matter of time before their eyes would meet and they would speak. She was sure of it, and her daily watchful ritual was enacted because of the possibility, nay the inevitability, of that encounter.

*   *   *

Doña Luz had squatted at the old ruin since the death of her mother three years before. Although the matriarch of the Martínez family was 97 years old at the time of her death, she had been of robust health and keen of mind and spirit until shortly before her death. When her ancestral family adobe had been bulldozed with the blessing of a progressive city council to make way for a multi-level parking garage in the inner city, she had died—some said of a broken heart—within a month of relocation to public housing on the city's far south side. (The urban renewal project had continued on schedule in spite of the fact that Doña Luz—always a spirited and independent woman— had, in a last desperate show of defiance, thrown herself down in front of the wrecking ball. This had resulted in a rash of negative publicity and a spate of sympathetic letters that had proved embarrassing to the city fathers. The furor died down within a few weeks, however, as the populace's short-lived attention span turned to more pressing matters like the World Series.)

Within a week of her mother's death, Doña Luz moved out of their one-bedroom apartment at La Reforma. The family heirlooms had been sold over the years to get through the hard times and to supplement Doña Luz's meager earnings as a folder and stacker at Haskell Linen Supply. Doña Luz's remaining tat-

tered possessions—clothing, bedding, an antique trunk, a woodburning stove, and a few pieces of weather-beaten furniture—
had somehow mysteriously and miraculously reappeared in the
one section of the abandoned convento ruins that still had a
portion of its roof intact. The city fathers, who had annexed the
site, chose to look the other way. It was considered an eyesore,
used by some as a dump and did not have potential for development in the forseeable future. They preferred to concentrate
their energies and attentions on other more potentially lucrative
and respectable areas of the city.

(Doña Luz had been well known to officials before her celebrated encounter with the wrecking ball. She had been, in her
more youthful and vigorous days, a thorn in the side of several
generations of bureaucrats and attorneys, having laid claim, with
faded documents and dog-eared deeds, to several acres of land
where the multi-story government complexes now stood in the
heart of the city. Needless to say, the Martínez claims proved
fruitless in spite of years of wrangling in the courts, their case
weakened by the passing of time, the mists of history, a dearth of
witnesses and a maze of legal and bureaucratic entanglements.)

Thus the weary city fathers were only too happy to ignore
Doña Luz's latest display of obstreperousness, satisfied that age,
infirmity and time had taken their toll on her senses. They were
wrong, of course, having no way of knowing that Doña Luz's
senses were intact, she having abandoned the fleeting awards of
politics and protest for what she considered to be more sublime
and spiritual matters. Nevertheless, her ghostly comings and
goings at the ruins disturbed no one, threatened nothing, and
they had received no complaints.

Mi casa es su casa.

*   *   *

Alma hunkered down into the torn plastic of the car seat,
closing her eyes and concentrating her thoughts, trying to stay
warm. For the air had turned suddenly colder now, and the
clouds, gathering speed, had slammed over the weakening sun

like a curtain being drawn. Like a room with its candles snuffed out, the orchard and the ruins lay suddenly in shadows. The clouds, blackened and tinged with purple, scudded across the blank sky like so many tall ships in a tempestuous sea.

When Alma at last opened her eyes, she was startled to see Doña Luz standing before her, extending a veined hand to help her rise. Doña Luz had made her way across the bramble-and-branch-strewn field soundlessly, like a ghostly dark cat on padded feet. The old woman's hair was completely white—long and wispy like spun sugar candy. It blew about her face like smoke that threatened to disappear with the quickening wind. She was dressed completely in black: her long dress of coarse homespun cloth hung down to her ankles. The style of the skirt and bodice was reminiscent of those Alma had seen worn by the stern-faced women in the treasured antique photographs of her mother. On her feet Doña Luz wore a pair of old-fashioned hightops with no laces. She wore on her shoulders a threadbare fringed and embroidered shawl of the finest woven silk—the only surviving heirloom of her family's more exalted and prosperous days. Her face was brown, fine-boned and high-cheeked, wrinkled with age and weathered with adversity. Her eyes, set deeply and far apart, were small and bright, and so dark that they seemed to have no pupils. In the sudden obscurity that had come unnaturally with the storm, Doña Luz's luminous eyes were the only beacons in the darkened fields.

"Ven, mi hija. Ya es la hora." Doña Luz addressed Alma in Spanish in an urgent, musical voice. In the many weeks of her vigil, Alma had prepared herself for this moment, and she was not frightened by the sudden apparition of Doña Luz. She grasped Doña Luz's bony arm to steady herself as she arose from her seat; she was surprised at its strength in spite of its weightless fragility. She walked with her silently across the fallow autumn fields to her dwelling place in the convento. The wind was roaring now, whipping the delicate and brittle branches of the fruit trees. The branches, threatening to snap, made a rasping protesting sound that rivaled the din of the wind itself. Before they were halfway across the field, the promised moisture came, not in the usual rain, but in unexpected, silent flakes of snow that fell so thickly that everything in the orchard was blurred as though seen through a cataract-veiled lens. By the time they reached the adobe shelter of Doña Luz, Alma was shivering with the wind and the blowing snow. Doña Luz pushed open the heavy hewn door of her shelter, and in the smoldering half-light of ancient kerosene lamps Alma saw what she thought were hundreds of giant tattered white moths pinned to the ceiling and the rafters and the walls, covering the sparse furniture, or fallen, ankle deep, flightless and abject, on the floor.

"Tú estás encargada de todo esto," Doña Luz whispered to Alma with a dramatic sweep of her hand.

Outside, the snow gathered at the curtainless windows like gauze. . . .

When Alma's eyes had focused and become accustomed to the smoky room, she distinguished through the haze, not moths, but shreds of paper on which notes had been carefully and laboriously written in a spidery scrawl.

Doña Luz continued to explain in a whisper: "This is the history of our people which I have gathered—the land grants and the homesteads and the property transfers; the place names of the mountains and the rivers and the valleys and the pueblos; the families and their names and their issue; the deeds, honorable and dishonorable; the baptisms, the weddings, the funerals; the prayers and the processions and the santos to whom they are directed; the fiestas, religious and secular; the milagros and the superstitions. She droned on in a cadence, and as she spoke, Alma, still grasping her bony hand and surveying with wonder the testament of Doña Luz, felt the warmth of that hand flow into her being like water being poured. "The recipes, the herbs and the cures; the music and the songs and the dances; the prose and the poems, the sorrows, the joys; the gain and the loss. This is my legacy. But I am old and failing. I entrust it to you lest it be lost and forgotten."

The wind continued to howl and the snow veiled the windows in white lace. . . .

Alma stopped to pick up several pieces of the tattered scraps that lay at her feet, each veined with the faint tracings of Doña Luz's careful script. Squinting in the opaque half-light she read: "On February 10, 1897, Don Jesús María Figueroa perfected the title of his three sections of land under the Homestead Act. He and his family settled in the fertile canyon of the Madrona Draw of the mountain range we call Los Rincones. He named it Rancho de Los Alizos because of the great trees that grew there. He built his home, corrales and a chapel. There three generations of Figueroas prospered, cultivating grain, vegetables and fruit and raising livestock. In 1939 the United States Department of the Interior, claiming eminent domain, expropriated the land. Before he left for town, the grandson of Don Jesús María Figueroa burned the buildings and the two thousand dollars he received in payment . . ."

Alma read a second note, her eyes straining in the ever-darkening room: "The feast day of San Isidro, the patron saint of farmers, is May 15th. A little statue of the saint is carried through the fields, the farmers and their families singing alabanzas, offering their humble crops and praying that this year's planting might be successful. This is his prayer:

> Señor San Isidro
> De Dios tan querido
> Pues en la labor
> Tu seáis mi padrino
>
> Fuiste a la labor
> Comenzaste a arriar
> Junto con los hombres
> Que iban a sembrar.
>
> Porque sois de Dios amado
> Y adornado de esplandor
> Bendecir nuestro sembrado
> San Isidro Labrador . . ."

And the thickening snow smothered the windows and the ruins like a shroud. . . .

Alma continued to read with a mounting sense of urgency now: "Here is written the corrido of the ill-fated race when Don Antonio Valenzuela lost all he possessed when his superior and beautiful horse 'El Merino' lost to 'El Pochi' at Los Reales in 1888.

> ¿Qué hubo, Merino mentado?
> ¿Qué siente tu corazón?
> ¿Por qué estás apachangado
> Cuando eres tú en el Tucsón
> El caballo acreditado
> Dueño de la situación . . . ?"

The unfinished song flew from Alma's hands when suddenly, and without warning, a tornadolike gust blew open the unlocked door of Doña Luz's hovel. The airborne flakes blasted in with a ferociousness, and then Alma saw, helpless and aghast, that the shreds of precious paper, in an avalanche of blinding whiteness, had metamorphosed into giant white moths again. They quickened with life and took to the air in a dizzying funnel of flight. Blowing snow mingled with blowing paper and rose and fell and then eddied into a blizzard of memories. And then the memories and the spirit of Doña Luz fluttered out the open door in a thousand swirling fragments in the direction of the south wind somewhere west of Aztlán.

The Legend of the Bellringer
of San Agustín

There was never a morning that the old man did not ring the bell. Before the sun came up, he roused himself from his humble bed in the little house that lay in the shadow of the great white church. He made a cup of strong coffee for himself and drank it with a piece of sweet bread. He rubbed his sleep-filled eyes, still heavy with dreams, and fell on his knees to say his morning prayers. Then the old man shuffled slowly across the plaza in the darkness. The little pueblo slumbered, still cloaked in night. The proud roosters slept on the rooftops. Cats and dogs yawned before the hearths. Birds twittered sleepily in the trees. Chickens stirred in the courtyards. And children dreamed. All the pueblito lay quiet with the expectation of the new and coming day.

When the old man reached the cathedral, he opened the massive carved doors with only the light of a candle to guide him. With the small flame he led himself up the winding stairs to the bell tower. There, in silent splendor, hung the magnificent bell of San Agustín. It was made of bronze, and had come from across the sea so long ago that no one could remember a time when it had not sung its song for the little town. It shone, even in the darkness, with a wonderful light all its own, and in the hush of the tower, it seemed to tell a story.

For on the magnificent bell there were all manner of marvelous creatures, forever stilled in bronze, yet looking as if someday they would come to life. Near the crown of the bell, beautiful women—or were they angels?—strolled under the branches of enormous trees, their faces forever fixed in metallic beatific smiles. Children played gayly along a silent and forgotten river where fish swam with eternal grace. Along the river, rushes bent before a secret wind, and birds of paradise strolled haughtily among the bronze flowers. Around the center of the fabulous bell, chariots raced on golden roads to an unknown destination. The men in the chariots—were they gods or kings?—no one knew for certain.

Every kind of animal—great and small—made its way around the bell of San Agustín. Butterflies and bees hovered in the gardens; mountain lions hunted in the woods; snails crawled in the grasses; deer pranced in the meadows. And on the rim of the bell, intertwined with vines and flowers, were written the words: ¡CANTAD AMIGOS! SING, FRIENDS! Yes, it was a grand and glorious bell, the bell of San Agustín.

And somehow the old man always knew just when the sun would stir from its night-veiled rest. And so, just before the first rays of light seeped over the hills, the old man grasped the great thick rope in his hands and pulled. He was a small man, and not strong, yet he pulled the ropes with ease. It was as if the angels themselves lifted him. He pulled the ropes, and the great bell swayed rhythmically in song. And the song sang of the shadowed mountains, and of the first morning light, and of the clouds that came with the new day. And the song sang of the hawks flying in the wind, and of the cottonwood leaves trembling in the breeze, and of the children dancing in the plaza, and of the river trickling in the sand, and of the coyote's lament to the moon. And with the first notes of the melody, the morning light broke over the Rincón Mountains. The dawn of the sun and the melody of the bell flowed like yellow honey and seeped into the windows and doors and eyes of the people. And the pueblito would awake with joy. The cocks crowed; the dogs barked; the doves called. Everyone sang: the maidens grinding corn; the children at their play; the vendors pushing carts; the farmer planting seeds at his milpa. . . .

Everywhere, when the celebrated bell of San Agustín sang, the whole world sang. But one morning the bell of San Agustín was silent. The old man climbed the stairs to ring the morning

Angelus, and never climbed down again. They found him with the bell rope still in his hands, his eyes forever closed in sleep, and on his lips an eternal smile. That morning the sun rose with a pallor and there was a grayness over the little town. There was no song from the bell, and there was no song from the people of the pueblito. For three days the bell did not ring, and for three days it seemed as if the sun and the town were in mourning.

The people of the pueblito began to ask themselves, "Now who shall ring the bell? The bell must be rung, or the town will die of sadness." And so they called together a committee to choose from among themselves a person who would ring the bell.

"We shall have a person who is strong to ring the bell," said Don Emilio Gallegos, the mayor. "For the bell is made of bronze, and it is very heavy."

"Yes, yes. The alcalde has decided wisely," agreed all the people. And so the mayor and townspeople chose Guillermo Flores, the blacksmith, to ring the bell. His hands were powerful and his arms were mighty. And so it was, that on the fourth day after the old man had died, Guillermo Flores climbed the bell tower of San Agustín to ring the famous bell. He took hold of the rope in his immense hands and pulled, but the bell hung in silence. He called up all his strength and pulled again, but the bell was still. At last Guillermo climbed down from the tower and met with the mayor and the people of the town. "It is no use, your honor, and my compadres. The bell will not ring."

The mayor and the people of the town then decided that it should be Don Leopoldo who should ring the bell. After all, was not Don Leopoldo the richest man in town, and the most influential? And so Don Leopoldo Romero was chosen to climb the dark and rickety stairs up into the belltower the following morning. All the servants from his household climbed with him, some carrying the train of his magnificent cape. When they reached the top of the tower, and when he gave his command, they all pulled on the rope together—the manservant, the maid, the gardener, the carriage driver, and Don Leopoldo. But to no avail. The great bell of San Agustín remained silent.

With each passing day that the bell did not ring, it seemed as if the pueblito grew sadder. The corn wilted in the fields; the birds languished in the trees; the bougainvillea did not bloom; the children cried themselves to sleep. The farmer no longer hummed on his way to his milpa; the maidens sighed at their metates.

So the mayor and the citizenry held another meeting in the plaza. The mayor, Don Emilio, said, "No one can ring the bell, because we have not made the correct choice. The bell must have a secret which we must decipher. So let us send Dr. García for he is the most educated and the wisest man in the village. He can solve the mystery of the bell." So Dr. García, laden with his books, and in the company of his advisers, ascended the dim tower before the sun came up that following morning. They read and discussed and philosophized. They debated and exhorted and explained. But when it was time to ring the bell, the bell would not chime. At last Dr. García climbed back down from the tower, muttering and pulling on his beard in vexation.

"A meeting! A meeting! We must have another meeting of all the people in the pueblo and from the surrounding ranchos!" announced the mayor. So that evening all the people gathered in the little plaza to decide what must be done about the ringing of the bell.

They argued and disagreed and worried. Some thought that Padre José should try next to ring the bell, for he was the most saintly. Some thought Señorita Aurelia Romero, because she was the most beautiful. And some voted for Don Diego Rascón, for he had traveled far and wide and was the most experienced in the matters of the world. The night wore on, the moon dropped below El Cerro del Gato, and still the people could not come to an agreement.

And while the people disputed and discussed, a little vaquero named Alfredo wandered down from among the hills that surrounded the little town of Tucson. He had been a vaquero all his life, and he was happy with his simple and peaceful ways. At night, with the quiet of the cerros whispering to him, he would listen in silence and reverence to the music of the universe. The winds sighed in the trees, and in the leaves there was a melody. The sleepless and errant mockingbird trilled its love song in the night air. The chirp of the crickets serenaded the moon. The cry of the coyote rang across the plains. The cattle stirred and lowed in the darkness. And the stars danced across the heavens in eternal rhythm. And every morning, for as long as he could remember, when the dawn star hung like a diamond on the peaks of the Rincón Mountains, the little vaquero played his guitar and joined the bell of San Agustín in the morning song. And together with the wind and the mockingbird and the cricket; and the coyote and the cattle and the stars; and the guitar and the bell, there was, on los cerros de las Catalinas, a symphony to the world.

And so it was, that when the bell of San Agustín had been silent a fortnight, the little vaquero thought to himself, "The bell of San Agustín has not rung, and I must serenade the morning star and the dawn without it. I will go into the town and climb the tower and ring the bell myself."

And so the little vaquero silently, and unheeded by the people, ascended the stairs to the belltower. In the half-light of the tower, he took the bell rope in his hands, a rope that had been worn smooth by the love and the labor of the old man. He pulled on the rope, and just as the sun rose in the East, the bell of San Agustín once again rang out its melody into the pueblito and the surrounding valley and hills.

When the joyful refrain reached the ears of the people in the plaza, they, together with the mayor and the other dignitaries of the town, ran to the church just in time to see the vaquero Alfredo coming out of the doors and descending the steps.

"Alfredo! Alfredo!" they all clamored at once. "It must be a miracle! How did you do it? How did you make the bell ring again? What is the secret of the bell of San Agustín?"

Alfredo looked at his compadres, the villagers. His eyes were shining with wonder. "The secret of the bell is this, my friends. The song is not in the bell. The song is in the heart of him who rings the bell. And the song is in the heart of the people."

Dreams

There was always an air of mystery about our grandfather—like a door slightly ajar to a dimly lit room full of secrets. My mother, whose own family had descended from proud but dispossessed gachupines, alluded as often as possible to his questionable past, but her bias, it seems to me now, had to do as much with the darkness of his skin as with his history. He was a renegade, she benignly hinted, a man on the run who had changed his name to hide from his deeds and the law. What his real name was we were never told—we knew him as Tata Elías—in fear, perhaps, that a childish slip of the tongue might bring the authorities.

In truth, we hardly knew the old man at all, for he paid scant attention to us and hardly spoke. He sat wordlessly at meals, chewing noisily or slurping caldo through his coffee-stained bigote. If he spoke, it was to complain—the soup was too hot, the coffee too weak, the meat too tough. He would eat slowly, deliberately, hunched over, intent on his plate, as silent and immovable as one of the apostles in the dime store print of the Last Supper that graced the wall above the kitchen table. Abuelita would flutter to and fro, between the table and the stove, at his beck and call. Tráeme esto. Tráeme lo otro. She, as loquacious as he was silent, her homemade frock dusty with harina, dark bright eyes darting, anticipating his every need, and every potential misdeed of her bad-mannered grandchildren. Mal Educadas. From time to time she would flutter her hands at us behind his back or place her finger to her pursed lips, in a last minute, desperate attempt to signal us lest we chatter or squirm or spill

27

and thus shatter his composure. This having failed more often than not, she would clasp her hands in prayer, roll her eyes heavenward, and beg the intercession of the aforementioned apostles. Nana Elías. A believer in miracles. Tata Elías's protectoress and oasis in the tangled garden of his self-imposed exile.

As for my sister and myself, we were as oblivious to the dreams and cares of the old man as he was to ours. We had become adept at dodging the discipline of his cane as we innocently disturbed his tranquility and shattered the delicate shell of his solitude. We slammed doors, teased his rooster, trampled his garden during the myriad games of childhood. Diabilitas. Malcriadas. Encimosas.

Except for mealtimes and naps, Tata Elías spent his days seated in an oversized chair made of pine and rawhide thongs that was placed under a ramada on the south side of the house. The chair, his most precious possession, was the only heirloom salvaged from his rancho in Mexico. It had been made to order for his tall and angular frame, but the years and pendientes and his losses had shrunk Tata's bones and he seemed lost, wizened and childlike in the oversized throne. Nonetheless, there he sat and surveyed his diminutive kingdom and brooded about his lost youth and strength, his prowess with horses and with women, his abandoned rancho of the rolling hills and the singing river. Now the parameters of his world were a tiny lot and house in Barrio Hollywood.

A carrizo break on the east side of the lot and a huge prickly pear fence on the west side shielded him from the prying eyes of the neighbors. At the far end of the lot under a salt-dusted tamarack was a ramshackle chicken coop inhabited by a one-eyed rooster with an evil disposition and his harem of forlorn hens in various stages of pecked disarray. Tata Elías kept watch over the motley flock as if they were a herd of high-strung racehorses or prize cattle. Every morning an egg or two or three would miraculously materialize in the nests of these dispirited pullets. This was Tata's domain; no one was allowed to enter the coop or gather the eggs but him. They were for his consumption alone: his manna from heaven, the bounty of his harvest, pearls of great price, the only precious stones remaining in the diadem of his monotonous days.

Day after day he kept his vigil over his chicken coop and the inhabitants thereof, watchful for intruders. Day after day he kept his vigil over his small vegetable garden with its undersized tomatoes and chiles and squash withered by the desert sun. He kept vigil over his stunted fig tree which struggled valiantly in the heat. His gray eyes blinking moistly, he kept vigil over the day's shadows as they kept pace and grew and faded with the sun. He would move his lips soundlessly hour after hour, in conversation with himself and long dead cronies, repeating to himself his own story, lest in the failure of the telling, he would finally and irrevocably vanish like a wisp of smoke in the autumn air. And the days rolled by like beads of rainwater on a pane, and the days pooled into the nostalgic corners of his mind and drowned him with his memories.

(Don Jesús Elías. Sí, que era muy hombre. Muy guapo y fuerte. Muy macho. No le tenía miedo a nada o a nadie. He sits on the black stallion tall and straight and handsome. Moreno. His chaps are made of tooled leather. His bridle and his saddle are trimmed in silver. His reata he braided himself from the mare's tail. His bigote is black and full. His sombrero is wide to shield him from the rain and the sun. He shouts his orders. He is the patrón. "¡Vaqueros! ¡Ya ándale!" There is the trample of the horses' hooves, and the longhorned cattle mewl and bawl and flow like a brown river down the escarpment of the green hill and across the boulder-strewn river. The cowboys curse and whistle and shout. The stallion rears and neighs, and Don Jesús Elías laughs and rides like the wind. The sun goes down. Three more days of roundup. The steers pace in the corral. The sweat of the men and the horses linger and mingle with the aromas of tobacco and coffee to perfume the night air. Don Jesús Elías rolls a cigarette. He strums his guitar and sings to the evening star and to Sylvianita of the raven tresses.)

> El potrero está sin ganado
> La laguna se secó

Ay, yay, yay, yay.
Y aquella casita
Tan blanca y bonita
También se perdió.

He skipped breakfast that morning, complaining of indigestion, and went to sit in his chair under the ramada as was his habit. He did not respond to Abuelita's calls to lunch. And thus they found him, in his customary position, facing South, gray eyes open, staring and glassy; mouth stiffly agape in an interrupted command; cane brandished and frozen in midair, pointing out something on the horizon. "¡Ya ándale, vaqueros!"

Earth to Earth

Part I: 1910

THIS IS THE WAY YOU MAKE ADOBES: You lie in bed sleepless, staring into the darkness of the ceiling shadows made mysterious by the moon, waiting for Mamá to call you to get up. The cock has not even crowed, but you know that Mamá has been a long time in the kitchen preparing the canasta of food for the day at the river. Through a crack in the door you can see the faint glow of the kerosene lamps. You can hear Mamá's determined footsteps, the faint rustle of her petticoats, and the snap of the mesquite leña in the woodburning stove. You can smell the aroma of all the bocaditos she has prepared for the día de campo. She has made flour tortillas and wrapped them in an embroidered cloth. She has made fried chicken and salsa de chile verde and frijoles con queso which will stay warm in a blue enameled pot. There will be sandía, too, and empanadas de camote, and limonada in an earthenware crock.

You lie impatient and expectant, but obedient. You know that if you get up too soon, Mamá will scold you for being an encimosa and getting underfoot.

Papá is in the corral hitching up the reluctant mare to the wagon. You can hear the stubborn mare snorting and stamping, and your father's soft clucking admonishments. At last you hear the creak of the wagon wheels, the clink of the bridle, and the mare's rhythmic plodding in the fine dust of the callejón. Papá

31

will hitch the mare to the ancient álamo by the gate and come into the house and begin loading the buckboard with provisions. He will not forget the guitar.

The glow under the door begins to fade as the bedroom fills with soft morning light. My twin brothers, flojos that they are, lie sprawled in their cot, snoring in unison, their arms intertwined like two rag dolls. As inseparable in their dreams as in their waking hours. The baby sleeps peacefully in her cradle, her cherubic face glowing in the dawn like a miniature replica of the moon that has now dropped below the western horizon.

(I remember well the evening Papá began hewing the cradle from rough-sawn pine boards. He worked rapidly, wordlessly, concentrating, his brow furrowed, the aromatic pine chips piling up at his feet. I knew that it would not be long before there was another López mouth to feed. I remember, particularly, his large veined hands with the long delicate fingers, the nails bruised from hammers that had missed their mark. His varnish-stained palms were flecked by the innumerable slivers of all the wood he tried to bend to his artistic will while he plied his carpenter's trade. He was, with all those slivers, half tree, half man, strong and tall and straight and silent—a forest of a man who provided sombra for all. And when he finished the cradle, Papá gave me a penknife and I carved a clumsy flower on the headboard, praying all the while secretly, that the new baby would be a girl. My wish came true, and they named her Margarita, like the flower I had carved that day. And all of my life, because of that flower, I have felt blessed.)

The door opens. Mamá calls in a whisper: "¡Otilia! ¡Levántate ya!" I spring from my bed, fully awake, being careful not to disturb my mischievous older brothers, jealous of my grown-up responsibilities and my time alone with Mamá and Papá. I dress hurriedly. Today I will wear faded dungarees and a shirt of homespun, and botas. Mamá will braid my hair with rags. No silly ironed curls with ribbons. No frilly starched dress or stiff patent shoes that pinch. No lacy anklets that leave itchy little ridges in my skin. No reminders to: "¡Bájate; cuídate; siéntate; cálmate; no te ensucies!" Today, Mamá, relaxed with her novela beneath the canopy of the cottonwood by the lulling river, a contented baby crooning at her side, will furl her banner and call a truce in her war against dirt and impropriety. And I will run free on the riverbanks, my trenzas unraveling, my boots abandoned and solitary in the crook of the tree. And I will catch frogs and June beetles and sail leaf boats and build castles of river mud and sticks.

Papá and the cuates will dig an earthen pit close to the river's edge. They will turn the clay-filled earth over and over with spades, mixing it with river water and straw. When I tire of play, I will roll up my dungarees to my knees and help, sorting out the large pebbles and then working the muddy mixture with my feet until it oozes between my toes. When the earth and straw and water are of the right consistency, Papá and the twins will hoist the laden buckets out of the pit and fill the rectangular wooden frames that form the adobes. I help tamp the mixture into the forms, smoothing the cool wet clay to the corners with my hands. I survey my handiwork and sign each one that I have made with the print of my bare foot. The frames are then set out into the sun to dry. In time, the cache of adobes, like giant terra cotta dominos, will grow until there is enough to make a wall. And then another wall. And then a room. And then another room. (Papá does not notice my footprints until the day he begins to lay the sun-dried bricks along the outline of the house marked with string. He laughs and lifts me high in the air with his sunburned arms. "These," he declares, "are for Otilia's house.")

When the day is done, I help load the wagon with the empty baskets and the pillows and blankets. While I wait for the others, I make a hiding place among the pungent straw and blankets. I inhale the sunset in great rosy breaths and try to pluck the evening star for my finger. Glad for the solitude, glad for the dove's lament, glad for the grillo, glad for the shining river, glad for the earth's turning and turning—the generous spinning earth that will yield up to us willingly, block by adobe block, room by adobe room, a new home on a barren lot on Anita Street.

*   *   *

"The Federal Housing Act of 1961 strengthened
the concept of urban renewal . . . Under the
Renewal Act, public acquisition of land would
be necessary. Consequently, when the area is
ready for redevelopment, and following two acquisition appraisals, the city proceeds acquiring
the land at 'its present fair value for present own-
ers.' Such an endeavor is accomplished by nego-
tiation, and if that fails, then eminent domain is
exercised. Land acquired is then sold to private
developers for its fair value after it has had two
re-use appraisals . . . Usually the return from the
sale to private developers fails to offset the acquisition, planning, clearance and off-site improve-
ment costs. One important reason is that the
land is purchased with structures which must be
removed."

Part II: 1973

The unexpected knock at the door causes Doña Otilia López,
viuda de Martínez, to suspend her knitting needles in midair.
Poised like that, the needles look ferocious, difficult to associate
with the confectionary of bonnets, booties and baby sweaters that
materialized out of their metallic clicking. Doña Otilia sighs and
places her latest project—yellow booties shaped like ducks—
into the sewing basket at her feet. For grandchild number fifteen.
Or was it fourteen? She always lost count. She glances at the
electric Westclox she kept centered on a crocheted doily on the
radio-phonograph console. The console, which her husband had
bought after the war, had not worked for years, but she had kept
it anyway, it being, in her opinion, her most elegant and practical possession. She stowed sweets for her grandchildren in the
turntable, yarn and thread in the record cabinet. The top of the
console served as the resting place, not only of the clock, but of

four generations of family photographs—antique sepias in ornate metal frames, black and white snapshots, technicolor wedding poses, blurred polaroid images.

(In a large handcarved frame of walnut, bedecked with two faded black ribbons, grinned the innocent and eager faces of the cuates dressed in jaunty sailor whites. They had enlisted together despite the pleas of Mamá. Twelve months later they would both be dead—propelled by a torpedo from the iron bunk they shared in the stern of the submarine. In step. Embracing in death as in life. When the telegram arrived, Papá planted two pine trees in their memory in the back yard. Two salt tamaracks grew there instead, from all the tears he shed that day. He did not speak for a year. And when he spoke, he said, "The house belongs to Otilia." And then, it seemed, the tree in him died. He grew frail and withdrawn, his trunk withered before its time, the leaves of his canopy dried and scattered by the winds of his grief.)

The trusty little Westclox hummed eleven. An unlikely hour for callers. Too early for lunch. Too late for café. Probably salesmen. Or Jehovahs. The Jehovahs persistent in spite of the fact that Doña Otilia's home altar, with its perpetually lit candles, was visible from the doorway, the array of saints, virgins, martyrs, and santos niños gazing sternly at any interlopers bearing unorthodox propaganda. The altar itself was not only a heavenly, but an earthly shrine as well. Mementoes of the rites of passage of Doña Otilia's family—funeral mass holy cards, baptismal and confirmation certificates, dried remnants from quinceañera and wedding bouquets, anniversary souvenirs—all were arranged lovingly among the santos and the plastic flowers from the five-and-dime.

Doña Otilia crosses the room, her chanclas slapping on the threadbare carpet. Her eldest son, Miguel, who had gone to night school and had done well for himself, had insisted, against her protests, on that carpet. He was muy de moda, up on things, and said it made the house more modern. Besides, it was for her own good. Throw rugs were dangerous. She might catch her foot and slip and break her hip, and that would be that. As she makes her way to the door, Doña Otilia notices for the first time that the

old wooden floor of pine planks that her father had so painstak-
ingly laid so many years ago was once more beginning to show
through the worn fibers of the cheap carpet. "Todo a su tiempo,"
she thinks to herself, satisfied. She had noticed too, lately, the
sagging roof, flaking paint and cracked plaster that exposed the
adobe walls of her house. She liked it that way, she mused, even
though Miguel was always worrying himself with painting, plas-
tering and repairs. But to Doña Otilia it was as if the house were
trying to reveal itself, throwing off its superfluous garments, like
an aging queen removing her makeup. She thinks about the
pitter-patter of her childhood footprints in the walls. She smiles.

Doña Otilia opens the front door. Through the latched
screen she can make out the blurred faces of two men. Both wear
dark suits and ties. (¡Qué simples! ¡En este calor!). Both are
perspiring profusely and mopping their brows with white mono-
grammed handkerchiefs. They shift from foot to foot, uncomfort-
able with the heat and with their unfamiliar surroundings. They
are not salesmen or Jehovahs. There are no wares or pamphlets.
They carry, instead, black briefcases that bode of something official. The scruffy little mongrel of Doña Amelia next door barks
ferociously from behind the broken slats in the picket fence. The
curtain at the window moves slightly as Doña Amelia positions
herself to get the best view and to hopefully be within earshot.
There will be much speculation and discussion of the strangers
over afternoon coffee. Doña Otilia chuckles to herself because
for once she will have the upper hand of the conversation.

The shorter of the two men speaks first, in halting high
school Spanish.

"¿Es Ud. Sra. Otilia López Vda. de Martínez?"

"Sí, señor."

"¿Es Ud. la dueña de esta casa?"

Proudly. "Sí, señor."

He raises his black briefcase and snaps it open, revealing the
contents: official forms in triplicate. The tall man then waves a
business card in his chubby fingers. Doña Otilia marvels at the
pinkness of his skin—the same color as the bonnet for grandchild

number nine. Or was it number ten? She squints at the card
through the screen, having left her reading glasses behind with
her knitting. The card is embellished with the blue and gold seal
of the city. It reads:

Donald K. Murphy   City of Tucson
Urban Renewal Project   Relocation Counselor
                Bilingual

*   *   *

"When the Old Pueblo's Urban Renewal Office
was first established, interviews were conducted
with residents of the area to be demolished. Pre-
liminary work on relocation problems was
mapped out. Thereafter, a marketability study
and reuse appraisal of the neighborhood were
completed. An eighty-two-member citizen's advisory redevelopment committee, which had
been appointed by the mayor, held its first meeting in October, 1969. At this time subcom-
mittees were formed to deal with planning, financing, relocation, legislation and public
information. In April, 1971, the city's advisory
committee adopted the subcommittee's report
and recommendations for planning for the Old
Pueblo District. The plan included a community
center with a music hall, theatre, and concert
arena. Later stages of the plan called for an office
plaza, condominiums, and a Mexican style village with restaurants and shops that would be a
tourist attraction. Upon approval by the mayor
and council, the financing of the plan was pre-
sented to the voters of Tucson who approved it
by an overwhelming majority."

Part III: 1976

Sam Morgan worked a toothpick in the gap between his front teeth to get the piece of bacon rind that had been stuck there since breakfast. After he had dislodged the fragment of pork, he continued to chew on the toothpick, moving it dextrously from one side of his mouth to the other. He did this habitually, hence his nickname, Woody. To his co-workers at Johnson Demolition and Salvage Company, the toothpick had become an integral part of his personality, like the Dallas Cowboys cap he invariably wore to protect his ruddy face from the sun. In spite of the cap, the sensitive skin on his nose was always peeling from exposure.

Morgan's back felt stiff that morning, and he kept shifting his position in the metal seat of the bulldozer, adjusting a cushion against the small of his back. He used his right hand to operate the shift lever and his left to steer the bulldozer into position, lining it up with the gaping doorway of the old adobe house he was about to raze—number 57 in his plot map. The doors and windows of the house, and anything else salvageable and salable like bathroom and kitchen fixtures and usable lumber, had already been removed, and the walls and the roof of the humble structure had begun to sag in acceptance and resignation. This one's gonna be a cinch, Morgan thought matter-of-factly to himself. Maybe he and the crew could take an early lunch.

It was only 9:00, and although he had had his usual big breakfast—four eggs, pancakes, bacon, orange juice and coffee—Morgan was already thinking about lunch. His wife had packed him his favorite—bologna sandwiches slathered with mayonnaise and Hostess Twinkie cupcakes to wash down with Koolaid. He was looking forward to not only his meal, but to the camaraderie of the noon hour. He and the rest of the crew could always find a shady spot under a big old tree on the Mexican side of town. They would sit in a semicircle, leaning against the rough bark and boast about women and fishing and argue about football. He had already picked out today's lunch site—two brooding tamaracks that towered in the empty lot behind house number 57.

Morgan was feeling lucky. Work had been steady since old man Johnson and his son had gotten a big contract with the city. Rumor had it that they had contributed generously to the mayor's re-election campaign, and rumor had it also that there were a lot of fat cat bankers and contractors who were very happy. But Morgan had no interest in the wheeling and dealing of politics or high finance. The relevant thing to him was that there were over 300 houses in 34 square blocks of city-owned land to be razed. It would take at least a year and it paid union wages and overtime. Which was a darn site better than working as a security man at the salvage yard out on the old Nogales Highway when there was no contract work. He disliked the tedium of the job, but what he disliked most was showing effete interior designers around, while they scoured the place for "antiques" and exclaimed over what Morgan dismissed as junk. That was woman's work. But operating the dozer took skill and being job foreman gave him status in his co-workers' eyes.

With the dump trucks and front loaders idling by, García, the flagman, signaled Morgan forward, keeping a wary eye all the while on neighborhood truants who might venture too close to falling debris. Morgan whistled the theme from "M*A*S*H" between the gap in his teeth and stepped on the accelerator. The bulldozer clanked and sputtered and spewed thick diesel smoke into the clear morning air. Morgan made a mental note to himself to spend a day overhauling it in the shop the next time they got rained out. With Morgan guiding it carefully, the dozer jolted forward slowly and at last met the wall of the old adobe with a resounding thud. The house shuddered but held. Morgan shifted into reverse and with García guiding him, backed up 100 feet to gain momentum. He lurched forward and rammed again. There was a loud crashing sound and then what seemed to be a suspension of all sound—a heart-piercing muting of men, children, engines, birds, dogs and idle conversation.

Then the old adobe house trembled, sighed, splintered, cracked and collapsed in on itself with a small explosion, enveloped in a shroud of dust that hid its final hour mercifully from view.

Then the dusty veil rose like fine powder into the golden morning air, carried aloft by a sudden westerly breeze from the river valley. The dusty cloud, catching the sunlight, gained momentum and floated over City Hall and the County Buildings and La Ramada Condominiums and the Federal Buildings and the Hilton Resort Hotel—until it settled, mote by golden mote, footprint by tiny footprint, on the parched and abandoned bed of the river.

María de las Trenzas

María Carmen del Castillo, like the summer sun that hovers just below the horizon, hesitates a moment before rising. She lies motionless, attentive, as if listening to distant music, her delicate hands folded on her bosom, her unplaited hair spread on her pillow like the undulating waves of a dark and stormy sea. A breeze makes the cottonwood by the arroyo tremble and moves the curtains of her open bedroom window. Already in that breeze is a portent of the day's heat which is to follow—like the warm elusive breath one feels in a crowded room. But for the moment, María savors the fleeting coolness of the morning and continues her waking dream . . .

(María, María, María de las Trenzas, her waist-length braids entwined with flowers and leaves, climbs the pyramid of chiseled stone at dawn. Its pinnacle is lost in haze from the surrounding lakes and expiatory fires. Its heaven-thrust altar shines crimson from the dawn and old sacrifices. And María, dressed in a flowing robe of white gossamer, bears the vestal flame and offerings of precious stones and her virginal self. The priest waits, arms upraised, obsidian dagger poised, his eyes bright and burning with secret knowledge. And the choral priests, robed in feathers, arms interlocked, chant and sway with soundless feet. And somewhere from beyond the shadows, the rawhide drums beat and call hypnotically: "María, María, María." And María climbs steadfastly, determinedly, toward the seductive echo, her heart pounding, her gaze unflinching, until she reaches the top of the pyra-

41

mid at exactly the same time that the sun breaks over the plain of
Tenochtitlán . . .)

María starts from her reverie when a sudden ray of brightness
flashes from her bedroom window. Once the sun rises in Barrio
San José, the heat accumulates relentlessly. Outside duties—the
garden, the chicken coop, the clothesline—must be attended to
before the sun reaches its zenith.

María sighs, dutifully crosses herself, and whispers her morning prayers. She rises slowly, placing her feet delicately on the
worn rug beside her bed. Her room is plain and unadorned,
almost cloister-like: a single bed, a straight chair, a bedside table
with a lamp and well-thumbed books, a cross on the wall. Her
dressing table contains the essential appointments and no more:
a brush, a comb, scissors, a can of dimestore talcum powder and a
jar of unscented handcream. Everything bespeaks a tidiness that
could only be the result of a singleminded devotion to order.

María stands and brushes the dark mane of her hair slowly and
thoughtfully. Then with delicate turnings of her fingers, she
twists her hair into two thick braids that fall below her waist.
Over her shoulders she slips on a shapeless cotton dress whose
flowered fabric has long ago faded with many washings. She
adjusts her feet into a pair of hard-soled slippers and noiselessly
goes into the kitchen. In the kitchen she uncovers the cage of
Julio, her canary, and freshens his paper, water and food. He
twitters sleepily and fluffs his feathers to catch the rays of sun now
streaming into his corner by the kitchen window. María then
places a teakettle full of water to boil on the stove for her father's
morning coffee. She then goes outside, being careful not to slam
the screen door and awaken her slumbering father before his
appointed hour. She steps out into the back porch, red-lined with
geraniums in cans, and in the rosy half-light of the morning, she
surveys her backyard kingdom, her gaze fixed on a distant and
indiscernable point . . .

(María, María, María de las Trenzas, astride a golden stallion,
rides a league ahead of the others, her raven hair loose and
streaming behind her, her grey eyes piercing the horizon. She
hears the sounds of the vaquero's voices in the distance, calling,

swearing, snapping their leather whips in the air; their saddles creaking, bridles ringing, chaps slapping against the heaving sides of their horses. And María is triumphant, because she has outraced them all. Her silver spurs urge the valiant horse to go faster, faster, and she laughs, parting her lips in short fast breaths, her fine white teeth showing. And María and the horse and the wind are one. And together they fly to the crest of the hill, and María unmounts and leans breathless and joyful against a fragrant and gnarled oak, her eyes following the red hawk that soars majestically on the wind currents over the verdant river valley . . .)

María awakens from her daydream as the dusty red hens peck impatiently at her feet for breakfast. She strews grain absent-mindedly before her, and then, shooing the jealous rooster, she goes into the lean-to coop and gathers four eggs which she nimbly places in the pocket of her housedress. Enough for Papá and for her for breakfast. She then irrigates a small vegetable patch slowly, thoroughly. The chile, tomato and calabaza plants are already festooned with miniature flowers that show promise of a late summer harvest. Next she waters the spreading and ancient fig tree and then the miguelito which grows in flowering pink profusion over the roof of the porch. Last she sprinkles a small garden of flowers, her mother's legacy—rose bushes, hollyhocks, stock and margaritas that grow in a jumble of color around a stone shrine of the Virgin in front of the house.

María then returns to the backyard porch and sorts laundry from a wicker basket. She fills the faithful old Maytag with a load of white linens—sheets, tablecloths and towels—adds a cup of soap and Clorox, and turns on the cycle. This completed, she reenters the house, taps lightly on the closed bedroom door of her father to awaken him, and goes into the kitchen to prepare him breakfast. It is the same fare every morning, for he is a man of habit: strong coffee laced with sugar and canned milk, huevos estrellados, papas fritas, and homemade tortillas warmed from the previous evening. María then sets the table methodically—pressed tablecloth, napkin, utensils, salt, pepper, and a bowl of chilitos encurtidos. Julio is now singing with exuberance, his

belly full, his feathers groomed, his pale yellow body warmed by
the sun now flooding his perch. The treble of his song rises and
falls, and fills and overflows the kitchen, and fills and overflows
María's silence. . . .

(María, María, María de las Trenzas, dressed in a gown and
cape of gold brocade and fur, stands poised in the brightness of
the light-flooded stage. Her upswept tresses are clasped in a
magnificent diamond tiara that reflects the light. The opera
house is full, hushed, expectant. María hesitates, takes a deep
breath, and then, with arms outstretched, sings the final aria.
Her voice soars to the balcony and to the vaulted ceiling, then
descends in a tragic tremolo of death and unrequited love. From
the glittering crowd there is stunned silence, a murmur, and then
thunderous applause. And María takes a sweeping bow and raises
her crowned and shining head to a shower of roses and the shouts
of ¡VIVA! ¡VIVA! ¡VIVA! . . .)

"Buenos días de Dios, María." "Buenos días, padre." María,
surprised from her fantasy, answers shyly, respectfully. Don Antonio del Castillo enters the kitchen, his newspaper tucked under
his arm. His freshly shaven face and perfectly starched and ironed
shirt and workpants are evidence of his abstemious grooming. He
is also a man of few words, having grown more taciturn since the
untimely death of his wife two years before. Don Antonio pulls a
chair out from the table, scraping its legs noisily on the linoleum
floor. He drinks his coffee with half-closed eyes, holding the cup
in both hands—hands stained, in spite of meticulous scrubbings,
from his labors as a mechanic in the Central Garage. He thinks
about his morning stiffness, the day's work ahead of him, and
how he misses his wife. He crosses himself at the thought of her,
glances at María, sighs audibly, and refills his cup. He feels
startled, when he gazes at María, to notice how much she resem-
bles her sainted mother: her fine-boned face, her luxuriant
tresses, her graceful movements. In all, that is, except her eyes.
His wife's eyes were brown and sparkled with laughter: a welcome
contrast to his own solemn countenance and demeanor. But
María's eyes are gray, unfathomable, changing in color and mood

with the weather and the light, always seemingly focused on some interior landscape.

Ah, well. Women. Who can pretend to understand them? He was grateful, at least, that his youngest daughter, his wife's namesake, had remained dutiful and foregone marriage and the vanities of the world to care for him in his widowerhood. His other daughters had provided him with grandchildren and heirs, it was true, but what peace can a man have in his life if there is no one to care for his house and his daily needs in his old age? Don Antonio finishes his breakfast while skimming the newspaper. He wipes his lips and his hands meticulously on the napkin and then folds the newspaper carefully along all the original creases. He would finish it after supper in his rocking chair in the sala—part of his daily ritual. He rises and takes a lunchpail which María has prepared for him off the kitchen counter. "Gracias, María." "De nada, padre." "Hasta luego. Que tengas buen día." "Gracias, padre. Igualmente." Don Antonio goes out the front door. María hears his heavy footsteps crunching on the driveway and the rattle of his truck as he pulls away from the curb. It is precisely 8:30.

María gathers and washes the dishes and places them on the dish rack to drain. She will sweep and mop and finish her kitchen chores after she has hung the laundry on the line to dry. She returns to the porch and piles clean wash from the Maytag into a plastic basket. She carries the heavy basket with wet linens on one hip, and walks to the clothesline at the back of the lot. She hangs the sheets and tablecloths and towels in three orderly rows until the lines are full. The sun has begun its relentless climb and reflects off the bleached linens with a dazzling brightness. It has already begun to get warm, and small beads of perspiration form on María's brow from her efforts. As she steps back to wipe her forehead and survey her handiwork, a sudden dustdevil that had been gathering momentum in the dry arroyo lifts the sheets and tablecloths into great flapping billows that swirl above María's head and block out the sun and the blank blue sky . . .

(María, María, María de las Trenzas, voyages on the great

ship on the endless sea. Its sails billow before the storm and bolts of lightning illuminate the green waves. And María, dressed in a gown of lace and deep blue velvet, her ebony curls pinned with pearls, waits in a mahogany-lined cabin lit by lamps of bronze. She hears the shouts of the men on the decks, fore and aft, blaspheming, giving orders, running with heavy clanking boots on the rolling slippery decks. And María prays, fingering a silver rosary with bejeweled hands. [I will be safe, yes, and the great ship will carry me to the shores of the New World where the viceroy is waiting in a palace of marble, for the King has so ordained.] And María of the luminous eyes is silent as she listens to the moaning and the creaking of the galleon . . .)

The creaking of the backyard gate interrupts María's thoughts. It heralds the arrival of Doña Margarita and Doña Josefa, grandchildren in tow, the first in the procession of her mother's comadres who come daily to visit and exchange milagros, recipes, cures, and tales of marital disputes or romantic intrigue. "Buenos días, María," they greet in unison. "Buenos días, Doña Margarita. Buenos días, Doña Josefa. Pasen. Pasen." The two señoras step onto the porch, the dark-eyed children clinging to their skirts. "¡Ay qué calor!" They fan themselves with their aprons. "¿No gustan café y pan dulce?" "Sí, gracias," they reply, already opening the screen door and stepping over the threshold into the cool interior of the house. (¡Cómo se parece a su madre! ¡Tan simpática y tan generosa! ¡Qué mujercita! ¡Qué casera! ¡Qué bendición a su padre!) By now the children have become emboldened and have scampered off to worry the hens or to play hide and seek in the alley. The damas seat themselves at the kitchen table and are soon joined by Sra. Martínez and Sra. Rodríguez. María brews a fresh pot of coffee and sets out a plate with pan de huevo. The litany of gossip begins in earnest now, punctuated by fluttering hand gestures and admonishments to the children who run in and out of the house chasing one another. ("No oíste que . . . ; Ay, pobre de . . . ; Déjame contarte . . . ; La hija de . . . ; Lástima que . . . ; ¡Válgame Dios . . . !") María continues working, deftly dodging children and personal questions. She sorts beans and puts them to soak,

roasts and peels chiles, mixes masa for the day's ration of tortillas, folds and mends, all the while half listening to the hypnotic
drone of conversation . . .

(María, María, María de las Trenzas, her wild mane of hair
covered by a homespun rebozo of many colors, sits at a table in a
darkened room heavy with incense. Flickering candles illuminate
the eager faces of the women who have come to seek her counsel.
Before her on the table lie bags of dried leaves and herbs and
flowers, boxes of ground powders and crushed stones, jars of
potions and unguents. She has collected them herself, by the
waxing and waning moon, sometimes walking for days without
sleeping in the mountain and river valleys. She speaks: "Wear
this stone in a pouch around your neck: it will guarantee love
from the most hardened of hearts; sprinkle this powder in lemon
and water: it will make you fertile; sleep with these leaves bound
to your forehead: they will banish your nightmares; scatter these
petals around your threshold: they will rid you of the mal de ojo."
Then María of the hooded eyes stands, and drawing a pair of
scissors from the folds of her rebozo, she cuts off long strands of
her tangled hair. She speaks again with a veiled voice: "And this
is the most powerful talisman of all. Wear a lock of my hair
pressed to your bosoms. It will unchain your fetters, help you
dream and put wings on your feet." Coins from the ladies' pockets
clink in a porcelain bowl—small recompense for the magic and
wisdom . . .)

María's trance is broken by the clink of dishes in the sink.
The comadres rinse their cups and saucers hurriedly, for the clock
in the sala has struck twelve, and they must wend their way home
to attend to lunch and their own household duties. María accom-
panies them to the front door to say adiós, and then returns to
her chair and the basket of mending in the kitchen. She threads a
needle, and with her head bent and her braids cascading over her
shoulder, she sews a button on her father's Sunday shirt. She
hunches her shoulders wearily as the day looms before her. The
weight of her duties is like the weight of her braids: more mending and sewing; washing and folding; scrubbing and dusting;
sweeping and mopping; errand-running and cooking. And the

evenings full of her father's absorbed silence rising to the ceiling like the smoke from his pipe. The only voice the one droning from the black and white TV. The only conversation the one between her father's creaking chair and the summer crickets that have escaped the scrutiny of her broom. Her only true companions the well-thumbed books that whisper their secrets to her during the long evenings in her room. Today like yesterday and tomorrow: all her days connected and identical like the dolls she cut from folded paper as a child.

María brushes back her heavy braids absentmindedly. She removes the newly sharpened scissors from the sewing basket, and concentrating, she deftly trims and snips fabric for the patch in her father's overalls. Her brow furrows in thought. There are no distractions now, only the warbling of the imprisoned Julio and the ticking of the clock in the sala. It chimes two o'clock . . .

*   *   *

Don Antonio del Castillo wipes his shoes carefully on the doormat and enters the house. He calls to María in greeting, but there is no reply. An emptiness, almost palpable, looms in the sala. He calls again. "María!" Silence. No cooking odors waft from the stove. Supper will be late. He goes into the kitchen, a scolding on his lips. The stove is cold; the frying pans empty. The cage door of Julio is ajar, the canary no where in sight. Don Antonio turns around, puzzlement on his face. And then he sees, coiled on the table by the window, the two long and luxuriant braids that María has cut neatly from the nape of her neck.

Days of Plenty, Days of Want

Part I

*En este mundo ni sobra el que viene
ni el que va*

Summer was the best season for Don Federico. The mornings were warm, and that meant he could start out before dawn with his horse, Benito, and his carreta, to buy fruit and vegetables from the Chinos at their truck farms by the river. It was convenient also, for at that early hour there was no traffic, and he could guide the carreta along a wide berth of the road without giving heed to the cars that were becoming more commonplace in the barrio since the war ended. The automobiles were noisy, meddlesome, created dust and fumes, and made his beloved and faithful Benito edgy.

Yes, the madrugada was the best time for the vegetable vendor. It was tranquil and he could concentrate on his thoughts without really watching the road—listening only to the melodious clink of his silver bridle and the steady rhythm of Benito's hooves until he reached the riverside milpas. The houses in the Barrio Anita were dark at that hour, except for the light in Doña Rosa's window. He knew she had already begun her morning devotions, lighting her candles on her home altar and moving her gnarled fingers rapidly along her clicking rosary beads.

"El hombre hace, y Dios deshace," she was fond of saying, and somehow it always consoled Don Federico to know that before sunrise Doña Rosa was attending to the spiritual emergencies at hand.

49

Sandía, melón, tomatillo, tomate, chile verde, cebolla, elote—the bounty of summer—these he would arrange in color-ful mounds on his carreta after bargaining for the best prices with the Chinos. Then he would make his way down the shaded cottonwood lanes back to the barrios on the edge of town—El Hoyo, Membrillo, Barrio Libre, and his own Barrio Anita—calling out to the housewives with his now familiar whistle and song: "Aquí viene la carreta de Don Federico; no soy ladrón. Cómprenme algo y les doy pilón."

He always made sure to have a bag of saladitos or dulces to give to the children who skipped, descalzos, after his carreta or hung from the silver bridle and clambered on the back of the long-suffering Benito, heedless of the scoldings of their mothers. If the morning was a good one, and the housewives in a buying mood, he would be home with an empty cart and a bolsillo full of coins before the scorching midday heat had set in. His afternoons he would devote to sharpening knives and scissors, to cutting firewood that was much in demand by the señoras for their estufas de leña, to cleaning the chicken coop and to tending to his own small gardens at the back of the lot.

Don Federico himself was a tall and slender man, moreno. He sat straight on the board seat of his homemade carreta, immacu-lately groomed, thanks to the tireless efforts of his sainted wife, Guadalupe. His shirt starched and spotless, if somewhat frayed, his khaki work pants perfectly pressed, his botas polished, he cut an elegant figure in spite of his humble demeanor, as if it were his calling to give orders to men instead of only to an ancient and trusted steed. His wife insisted he wear a felt hat to ward off the summer heat instead of the wide-brimmed sombrero which he preferred. "El hábito no hace al monje," he would remind her. But she felt it undignified and beneath his station. Poor they were, it was true, but of pioneer stock, gente de razón, here before the Gadsden Purchase, she was fond of recounting to anyone in earshot. Why at one time the Sotomayores owned great ranchos with thousands of hectares from the Altar to the Avra Valley. But because of the great drought, the greed of the "Americanos" and legal skulduggery, she was sure, they had lost

it all. "Papeles hablan; callen barbas"—and she had the pergamino to prove it, its faded proclamation scarcely legible, the
yellowed parchment transparent with age and handling.

The pergamino and other memorabilia she zealously guarded
in a wooden box which she kept under their bed: a linen cross-
stitch sampler ("En tus apuros y afanes, acude a tus refranes",
1850), a lace handkerchief, a gold pocketwatch with missing
hands and a cracked crystal, a leather-bound libro de oraciones,
and dozens of faded photographs and tintypes of dour men in
morning coats and prim women in yards of taffeta and lace.
These she would take out on occasion, arrange on the kitchen
table and reminisce about their turn of fate to anyone—pariente
or comadre—who would listen.

Don Federico would listen to his wife patiently when his turn
befell him. She was hardworking, devout, and most importantly,
a loving madre y esposa, and he felt she merited the luxury of her
nostalgia. But he himself was a practical man and there were
more urgent asuntos at hand: five children still at home to feed
and he not getting any younger. History interested him not as
much as the weather, the crops, and the dispositions of the
Chinos and the housewives.

Practical in all matters save one. There was one herencia
Doña Guadalupe did not safekeep in the locked wooden box
under their matrimonial bed. It was an herencia Don Federico
kept for himself or, mejor dicho, for his horse, Benito, and it
hung on a nail on the adobe wall of the sala when not in use: a
silver bridle intricately worked by some forgotten craftsman,
etched and embossed with a design of great beauty, leaves and
flowers intertwined, inscribed with the initials J.A.S., its original owner and history vanished like the land.

It was Don Federico's only indulgence, and sometimes, he
worried, an object of too much vanity. When the obligations of
the day were done—the produce, the leña, the sharpening stone,
the quarrelsome gallo, the gardens, the evening rosary—Don
Federico would light a kerosene lamp and go out to the makeshift
stable that housed Benito Juárez. There, seated on a stool made
from a discarded kitchen chair, and bathed in the soft light of the

lamp, he would groom Benito, unplaiting and brushing and re-plaiting his mane and tail, currying his hide until it shone, and rubbing the horse's aging muscles with salve. Then last, but not least, he would polish the wondrous silver bridle by lamplight, using a soft cotton cloth that he saved expressly for this purpose, shining it until the silver became warm in his hands and gleamed, its luster catching the light from the lantern like a thousand tiny stars. His wife would scold him if he stayed too late in the stable; it was foolish, she said, to lavish so much time on an old horse and bridle, and he so weary, too, of late. The bad evening air would surely give him the evil humors and he would catch his death from a chill.

Perhaps she was right, he would think on occasion. It is likely a sin of vanity. But then again, Padre Eufrasio at the Sagrada Familia Church had assured him in his Easter confession that it is holy and proper to attend to and admire all of God's works. The innocent Benito is also much loved by El Señor; and as for the silver bridle, it is the product of a God-given talent and so manifests the Maker's greater glory. And so, with the whispered words of the kindly old priest and the daily intercessions of Doña Rosa, the conscience of Don Federico was put at ease. . . .

The last morning was like all the other mornings. Don Federico arose in the darkness, being careful not to disturb his sleeping wife. He dressed in the clean clothes she had laid out for him the night before. He warmed his coffee, slipped the precious bridle from its nail hook, and still sipping from the steaming cup, walked out to the stable to the waiting Benito. He slipped the bridle over Benito's head, adjusting it just so, all the while whispering to himself his morning prayers. He harnessed Benito to the carreta, opened the creaking gate and began to make his way down the callejón to Otero Street and thence to the river, all the while listening to the musical sounds the bridle made, silver clinking upon silver, like miniature bells keeping time with the rhythm of the horse. He watched for the first rays of dawn to be reflected on the bridle's silver surface. Later he mused, the bridle would shine with a yellow light, almost like gold, the late morning sun the alchemist. Then the high noon sun would make the silver bridle flash with a blinding light that made him avert his eyes, a white and angular piercing light: like the pain between his ribs now that caught him so unaware that he let the reins drop from his hands with a sudden jerk. A flashing heart pain in his chest, silver almost, hot like a thousand suns, with tiny points of light fading into the distance and then going out one by one by one, like tiny candles in the wind.

Part II

Lo que viene volando, volando se va

Federico Sotomayor, "El Freddie," "El Huilo," unstacked the produce boxes in the room at the rear of El Grande Supermarket. It was always dark in the storeroom behind the swinging wooden doors. It was damp, also, with small puddles of standing stagnant water all around, and it smelled of overripened fruit and vegetables and insect spray. Later in the morning, after prying open the wooden crates, Federico would place them on a metal cart and roll them out to the produce section in the front of the store. There, washing them with the fine spray from a nozzle and sorting the damaged ones as he went, Federico would arrange the fruit and vegetables in colorful pyramids in the cases. When El Chino Lee was very busy with the afternoon trade, El Freddie would help out at the second cash register, while El Chino kept an eye on him all the while, making sure that no pilón escaped his scrutiny; that no unwarranted coins left the till. El Freddie liked this part of his workday best; he liked answering the questions of the señoras who wanted to know if that or this was in season, if this or that was fresh, and why the prices kept going up. He liked waiting on the barefoot children who came in with their centavitos to buy soda and potato chips. He always managed to slip the buquis a saladito or dulces if El Chino was distracted and deviated his ever watchful eye. Yes, El Freddie would think to himself: I am good with vegetables and people.

El Freddie walked twelve blocks from his house at 800 North
Anita to the Chinos. He would leave his carrucha at home to
save on gas and to protect his prized possession from the elements, to say nothing of prospective vandals and joyriders. He
would walk, mornings and evenings, at a leisurely pace, crossing
the river that was dusty now and crisscrossed by an eight-lane
freeway. The traffic drone never diminished in the barrios now.
The hum of trucks and cars had become a part of everyone's
consciousness, like a huge concrete insect buzzing in the ear day
and night.

But he liked the walk anyway; there was always something
going on in the barrio. People coming and going; toda la bola
hanging out after hours around the Anita Street store. "¿Qué
onda, Huilo?" A chula or two to eye. "Ay te watcho." Cooking
smells wafting from the kitchens into the streets; buquis playing
kick the can or softball in the dusty alleys and weed-strewn lots at
all times of the day or night; the abuelas rocking on their porches
exchanging remedies and milagros.

El Freddie's days were long—sunup to closing—Sundays too,
with Saturdays off. But El Freddie did not mind working overtime. More work meant more feria and more feria meant helping
out his old man and lady with what they needed to run the house.
More overtime meant more left over for fixing his carruchita,
which he parked in a makeshift garage he made from old boards
he had found at the back of the lot.

El Freddie's mother, hardworking that she was, with five
younger mouths to feed and never enough money to go around
with the mines on strike again, fretted about her son's spending
so much time working on his car. But she had faith and she kept
her complaints to herself. He was a good son—wasn't he?—
giving most of what he earned to make ends meet, and he was
practical in all matters save one.

Late at night, after warming the left over supper his mother
had saved him, El Freddie would work on his '53 Chevy. He had
strung an electric cord from the house to the garage and often
worked well past midnight by the light of that one bare bulb. The
car had been a junker-heap when he bought it from the gabacho's

wrecking yard on South Twelfth Avenue. Anybody can buy a new car, man, you take out a loan. But to transform a ranfla was a matter of orgullo, respeto, and raza pride. You work hard and create something a little different from anyone else. It takes a little time, a little talent, plus lots of patience, bloody knuckles, and some greasy levis. But mostly work. The more you work, the nicer your ride becomes. The more you work, the less time you have to get in trouble.

He had rebuilt the engine, doing most of the work himself, scouring the junkyards for parts and accessories, looking for a bargain. He saved his extra feria to pay for what he could not do himself. In three years the car was a masterpiece: multicolor lacquer paint job, chain link steering wheel, crushed velvet up-holstery on swivel chairs, spotlights on the hood, metal spoke wheels. The back window was etched with Carnales Unidos. ¡Ay, ay, qué firme carrucha! And hanging from the rear view mirror along with some fuzzy dice, were five sterling silver medal-lions attached to a worn leather strap, the largest of the medal-lions inscribed with the initials J. A. S. A gift from his old man, something handed down in the family, he said.

Late into the night he would work, tuning the engine, check-ing the batteries, polishing the chrome and buffing the finish with a leather shammy, the luster catching the light from the bare bulb like a thousand tiny stars. He would be looking forward to Saturday. . . .

That Saturday afternoon was like all the others: El Freddie all decked out in his khakis and plaid shirt and tapita, checking himself out in the bathroom mirror, shining his two-tone shoes on the back of his pants. Backing his carruchita out down the alley, slow, the buquis hanging on the bumpers, down to Otero Street and then to South Sixth to join the other vatos locos in the procession on the Avenue. Low and slow and mean and clean. Not a care in the world. The chulitas staring and the white guys too, with envy. Mi orgullo me levanta. His window was always rolled down to catch the breeze and to get a better look. The silver medallions on the rear view mirror flashed with the last rays of the afternoon sun.

He didn't even see the chota running down the sidewalk, with gun drawn, after the hippie who had taken off out of the Ozark Bar. Then he felt the bullet in his shoulder, and the pressure in his neck that caught him so unaware that he let his hands drop from the steering wheel with a sudden jerk. A white and angular and piercing pain, silver almost, hot like a thousand suns, with tiny points of light fading into the distance and then going out one by one by one, like tiny candles in the wind.

DIOS DA Y DIOS QUITA, ESE.

The Farewell

The six sons of Alfonso Santos, dressed in winter suits, too warm for the early Arizona spring. The six sons of Alfonso Santos carry the unadorned wooden coffin of their father down the narrow path to the cemetery in a place called the Tanque Verde. They perspire in the high noon sun, beads of moisture forming on their lips and forehead, their backs and arms dampened with sweat. Only yesterday the six sons of Alfonso Santos had cut the high spring grass and weeds of the easement, and the growth smelled sweeter and more pungent with each footfall of the funeral procession: the six sons of Alfonso Santos, fatigued with labor and grief; the six daughters of Alfonso Santos, they of the sad green eyes; and amigos, compadres, familia—viejitos mostly. Remnants of the old settlement who had lingered on and those who had gone away, but not forgotten, the place of their youth called the Tanque Verde.

> A spadeful, Padre,
> For the bygone days
> That we remember:
> A river that once ran sweet and true
> That watered our milpas
> And refreshed our souls.
> A river that flows no more.

The procession follows noiselessly along the trail now bordered by a barbed wire fence marked intermittently by signs: FOR

SALE: FIVE BEDROOM RANCHETTE WITH POOL; PRIVATE PROPER-
TY; NO TRESPASSING; BEWARE OF THE DOGS. The said dogs break-
ing the holy silence with their barks of warning, backs ruffled,
tails straightened; nervously pacing, kicking up little puffs of
dust, their yellow eyes on potential intruders.

> A spadeful, Padre,
> For the mesquite groves
> Where we ran wild as brown fawns.
> We played blindman's buff
> Racing barefooted with our eyes closed
> And never missed a step.

At last the funeral procession reaches the creaking cemetery
gate. NO FUNERALS ALLOWED. PRIVATE PROPERTY. The crowd
passes under the painted wooden arch, heads bowed in respect to
the final resting places of their families and friends. Weathered
wooden crosses, plaster of Paris saints and eroded faces, faded
plastic flowers, half-melted candles, and wrought iron crucifixes
are scattered in disarray. For death is never planned. Names
barely legible, if at all. Many of the graves unmarked, eroded
mounds. But the viejitos know the roll call: Figueroa, García,
Galván, Miranda, Bustamante, Valenzuela, Carrillo.

> A spadeful, Padre,
> For Carrillo's horse
> The one with the wild eyes
> Whose name was like the wind.
> And for Carrillo himself,
> Of the silver bridle
> And laughter like music
> And a smile like the sun.

NO FUNERALS ALLOWED. There had been negotiations, of
course. The six daughters of Alfonso Santos, they of the chestnut
hair, had sat for hours in the family room of the rambling modern
ranch house of the Johnson family. Fingering glasses filled with

instant iced tea, they spoke with heads bowed, in hushed voices. Yes, they were aware that the old community cemetery was now private property. Yes, they understood that there had been problems with trespassers, vandals, and curiosity seekers. Yes, they knew that there were no funerals allowed there any more. But please as a last request, could they lay their father to rest between his first wife, Guadalupe, the mother of all his children, and his second wife, Mercedes, who had raised the twelve sons and daughters after their mother's untimely death. And they would give up their own rights to be buried in the family plot. IN PERPETUUM. It was agreed. The understanding Americanos sealed the pact with a handshake.

> A spadeful, Padre,
> For the giant cottonwoods
> As old as the world.
> Our childhood refuge
> In joy and in sorrow.
> Branches like arms to hold us close
> Like our mother
> When she was gone.

The six sons of Alfonso Santos rest their precious burden on a sawhorse made of wooden planks, close to the yawning grave. They had dug the grave themselves, working through the night with borrowed shovels. A gnarled mesquite provides shade for the gathering mourners and sweetens the afternoon air with its fragrance, its perfume mingling with the faint incense still lingering on the robes of the deacon. A breeze wafts through the new green leaves and blossoms of the mesquite and cools the brows of the mourners, blowing its sweetness towards the brooding purple mountains. A melancholy dove calls from its hiding place in the thicket. Its dirge is as old as the prayers intoned by the deacon.

The deacon prays in English, quickly, nervously. The viejitos respond in Spanish. The deacon shakes a few hands, self-conscious, embarrassed. He moves to the shade of a tree and lights a

cigarette. He is wise. He knows that some things are best left
between a man, his children, and God.

> A spadeful, Padre,
> For the days that you were gone
> And we never knew where.
> And we lay listening to the night sounds:
> The coyote's cry
> And the groaning of the wind
> And our mother's soft sighs.

The six sons of Alfonso Santos lower the pine coffin of their
father into the waiting grave. They strain with the weight placed
on the ropes, their arms, now bare, rippling with exertion. The
six daughters of Alfonso Santos circle the grave like a wreath of
flowers.

It is finished.

> One hundred spadesful, Padre,
> For a place called the Tanque Verde
> Where the river runs no more
> And the fields lie fenced and fallow.
> And the giant trees, strangling
> Send their roots deeper and deeper.
> And the adobe houses have melted
> Back into the earth
> And the people have melted
> Into the city.
> One hundred spadesful, Padre,
> ADIÓS.

The Journey

In the warm and sun-filled days
I remember in the haze
The happy sounds of children laughing
The rustle of cottonwoods.
Now all is gray and cold and dark
Underneath Presidio Park.

The bell rings, the bus slows, and finally stops. I get off at the
corner of Fifth and Congress.

THE MARTIN LUTHER KING JR. APARTMENTS. ELDERLY PUB-
LIC HOUSING. Yellow and gray concrete walls six stories high.
Honorable Mayor James M. Corbett, Jr. Honorable Councilmen
Richard Kennedy, Kirk Storch, Conrad Joyner, Rudy Castro, and
John Steger. *Anno Domini* 1982-1983.

I go through the double-wide doors. The high-ceilinged waiting room is painted "robin's egg blue" (to make it seem cheerful).
The room is bare except for a few chairs and coffee tables clut-
tered with tattered magazines: *Good Housekeeping*—"Decorate a
Bedroom with Sheets." *U.S. News and World Report*—"The Ef-
fect of Arab Oil Prices on Wall Street." *Cosmopolitan*—"How to
Tell If Your Husband Is Faithful."

The black-and-white TV drones in the lobby. No one watch-
es it. The elevator clanks along noisily. (Up; Down; Press Button
Only Once.) A few viejitos are coming and going with purpose.
Some are waiting for the mail. DO NOT TALK OR INTERFERE WITH
THE MAILMAN WHILE HE SORTS MAIL. STAND TEN FEET FROM

61

HIM AND WAIT. Some are waiting for visitors. Some are just waiting.

And Tía is there, as always every Saturday, summer or winter, spring or fall, for the last two years. Except when the weather is too cold or too wet. It can never be too hot. Her small delicate figure is nearly lost in the big overstuffed chair. Tía is waiting for me. Quietly, primly, regally, her hands folded in her lap. She is wearing a shawl and a small knit hat. A flowered print dress and black stockings and shoes.

"Ah, m'hijita, ya llegaste." I take her arm, and she rises to her feet, not without difficulty. On one arm she carries a straw bag, and on the other a worn black umbrella, just in case. We walk slowly out the wide glass doors (EXIT HERE ONLY) into a late morning sunshine.

"Qué bueno que llegaste temprano. Tengo mucho que hacer, y la tienda está lejos. It is good that you arrived early. I have a lot to do, and the store is far away."

We begin to walk. Our journey. Every Saturday she insists on taking the same route. Across town. Down Congress Street. Past the Crescent Smoke Shop. (CIGARS, CIGARETTES, MAGAZINES, CANDY, PAPERS.) Past the Chicago Music Store. (TERMS, TERMS, TERMS, SE HABLA ESPAÑOL.)

Past the empty store windows with the dusty, limbless mannequins. We walk slowly, without talking. We turn on South Sixth Avenue, past the numerous bars and liquor stores. A hippie plays a guitar for quarters in front of Pete's Lounge.

We walk past Armory Park. Winter visitors are playing shuffleboard in the sunshine and winos are sleeping in the grass. On Ochoa Street, we turn west again and walk toward the gleaming white towers of San Agustín Cathedral. The pigeons flutter over our heads as the noon bells chime.

Señor Enríquez, the old bell chimer, died long ago. He climbed the rickety stairs to the bell towers three times a day for more years than anyone could remember. One day he climbed up and played the noon Angelus and never climbed down again. They found him with his eyes open to his last vision, a smile on his face, the bell rope still in his hands. Now the Angelus is a recorded announcement.

Tía laboriously climbs the concrete steps to the vestibule of the cathedral. I open the heavy carved doors for her and she makes her way into the cool darkness. The perfume of the incense from the early morning funeral Mass still lingers in the air. (Señora Juanita Rodríguez. Guadalupana. Sentinela. Legión de María. 6th Generation. Late husband, Miguel, was the founder of South Main Print Shop. Nine children. Twenty-seven grandchildren. Thirty-three great grandchildren.)

Down, down, the long corridor Tía walks until she reaches the side chapel of the Virgen de Guadalupe. La Madre de Nosotros. La Reina de Las Américas. She lights a small vigil candle and prays for the souls of husbands and brothers and sons. The ones who have died or lost their souls in Los Angeles. Father Carrillo walks by, intent on something. Cuentas y almas. Bills and souls. El Padre. Son of Barrio Anita. The pride of the people. "¿Y cómo estás, Doña Esperanza?" He grasps her hand warmly. She signs herself with his blessing.

We walk out once more into the brightness. Past an elegant old home that is now a funeral parlor. Down South Church and west on Cushing Street. Nearby a sign says: ENTERING BARRIO HISTORICO. HISTORIC DISTRICT. TUCSON—PIMA COUNTY HISTORICAL COMMISSION. In bronze. Many of the houses in the Barrio Histórico are owned by Stephen Peterson, a millionaire automobile dealer and amateur anthropologist. THE CUSHING STREET BAR AND RESTAURANT. Eat, drink and be merry in the authentic restored old adobe of the pioneer Ortiz family.

A sign has gone up on one of the old Soto houses. AMERICAN WEST GALLERIES—PRIMITIVE ANTIQUES.

"They tore down the Otero house," Tía says in Spanish. "They had a piano. The señora played beautifully. Everyone would come to listen. People would leave flowers on her doorstep. On Sundays, we would all walk down for the paseo in the plaza of the cathedral. Sometimes we would walk down to the river. (It had water then! Can you believe that the Santa Cruz had water?!) In the summers we would picnic under the cool shade of the cottonwood trees. Everywhere there was music."

Still on Meyer Street. Señor Romero is sitting on his porch reading *El Imparcial* from Hermosillo. He pays his rent now to Coldwell Banker, based in New York.

"Buenas tardes, Doña Esperanza."

"Buenas tardes, Don Felipe."

We walk on, slowly. Tía continues. "His father and his grand-father had tierras by the river. Everywhere it was green. They grew flowers and vegetables. And oh! the flowers! The perfume was everywhere in the summer breezes. His father, Don Enrique, sold vegetables from a cart. All of us children would run after the cart. He gave us free sugar cane. Now the river is dry. The milpas are gone and the people are gone. (The river had water then! Can you believe that the Santa Cruz had water?!)

The freeway has cut the river from the people. The freeway blocks the sunshine. The drone of the traffic drowns out the people's songs. A new music in the barrio.

On down South Meyer. At last we arrive. Lucky's Meyer Avenue Market. Tía opens the screen door. RAINBOW BREAD IS GOOD BREAD. "Buenas tardes, Doña Esperanza."

"Buenas tardes."

Tía fills her bag. The ancient cash register rings and whirs. Queso blanco, salsa de tomate, Campbell's Chicken Noodle Soup. White bread, tortillas de maíz, tortillas de harina, Cheerios. Pan mexicano, coffee. Saladitos for me.

"Gracias, Doña Esperanza. Hasta luego."

Then around the corner. Down South Main. Past the shrine of El Tiradito. THIS SITE IS ON THE NATIONAL REGISTER OF HISTORIC PLACES. TUCSON HISTORICAL COMMISSION. ARIZONA HISTORICAL SOCIETY. I follow unquestioning. I know that the journey is not over. There is always one more destination. Toward the Tucson Community Center. The Pride of Tucson. MUSIC HALL. LITTLE THEATRE. CONVENTION HALL. CONCERT ARENA. URBAN RENEWAL. Honorable Mayor Lew Davis. Honorable Councilmen James Corbett, Jr., Héctor Morales, James Murphy, Jim Southard, G. Freeman Woods and Kirk Storch. *Anno Do-*

mini, 1981. Concrete walls, and steps, and fountains. Fountains, fountains, everywhere. (The river had water then! Can you believe that the Santa Cruz had water?!)

Tía's pace quickens now. I follow her, carrying the straw bag laden with groceries. We walk past the Concert Hall to the vast Community Center parking lot. A billboard reads: CONCERT TONIGHT. ALICE COOPER. SOLD OUT. We stop in the middle of the parking lot. The winter sun is warm. The heat rises from the black asphalt. The buzz of the freeway is even louder. It is the end of the journey. I know what Tía will say.

"Aquí estaba mi casita. Here was my little house. It was my father's house. And his father's house before that. They built it with their own hands with adobes made from the mud of the river. All their children were born here. I was born here. It was a good house, a strong house. When it rained, the adobes smelled like the good clean earth."

She pauses. She sees shadows I cannot see. She hears melodies I cannot hear.

"See, here! I had a fig tree growing. In the summer, I gave figs to the neighbors and the birds. And there—I hung a clay olla with water to sip from on the hot summer days. We always had a breeze from the river. I had a bougainvillea; it was so beautiful! Brilliant red. And I had roses and hollyhocks and a little garden. Right here where I am standing my comadres and I would sit and visit in the evenings. We would watch the children run and play in the streets. There was no traffic then. And there was laughter everywhere."

"Ah, well," she sighs, "ya es tarde. It is time to go." I turn to follow her and then turn to look once more to the place where her casita once stood. I look across the parking lot. I look down. "Tía, Tía," I call. "¡Venga para acá!" She turns and comes toward me. "Look!" I say excitedly. "There is a flower that has pushed its way through the asphalt! It is blooming!"

"Ah, m'hijita," she says at last. Her eyes are shining. "You have found out the secret of our journeys."

"What secret, Tía?"

"Que las flores siempre ganan. The flowers always win."

We turn away from the sun that is beginning to drop in the West. I take her arm again. There is music everywhere.

> *Refrain*
> Abuelita, Abuelita, Abuelita
> No llores.
> Que te traigo, te traigo, te traigo
> Una ramita de flores.

Acknowledgments

"The Legend of the Bellringer of San Agustín" first appeared as an illustrated, bilingual-format booklet published by Pajarito Publications (Albuquerque, New Mexico) in 1980 as a Special International Year of the Child Publication.

"Earth to Earth" originally appeared as "Tierra a tierra" in *Saguaro* (Mexican American Studies and Research Center, University of Arizona, Tucson) 3 (1986):29–36. Quotations were adapted from "A Study to Identify and Assess the Psychological Ramifications Inherent in the Process of Relocation Regarding Census Tract I in Downtown Tucson, Arizona," by Patricia J. Clark and Martha M. Fimbres (master's thesis, Arizona State University, 1978).

"María de las Trenzas" won second prize for short story in the Chicano Literary Contest, University of California, Irvine, in May 1986.

"Days of Plenty, Days of Want" originally appeared as "Días de más, días de menos" in *Saguaro* (Mexican American Studies and Research Center, University of Arizona, Tucson) 2 (1985): 65–71.

"The Journey" originally appeared in the *Arizona Daily Star* (Tucson), February 4, 1979.

About the Author

Patricia Preciado Martin is a native Arizonan and lifelong Tucsonense. She is an honors graduate from the University of Arizona and has been active in the Chicano community of Tucson for many years.

Her books include two collections of oral history, *Songs My Mother Sang to Me: An Oral History of Mexican American Women* (1992) and *Images and Conversations: Mexican Americans Recall a Southwestern Past* (1983), both published by the University of Arizona Press, and her work has been included in numerous anthologies.

She lives in Tucson with her husband, Jim, and counts the hours until her children visit.